To my nieces and nephews, who need a better story —BL

For Kai —MG

ABOUT THIS BOOK: The art for this book was created in watercolor, pen and ink, and gouche, as well as digitally. This book was edited by Susan Rich and designed by Jamie W. Yee with art direction by Saho Fujii. The production was supervised by Ruiko Tokunaga, and the production editor was Marisa Finkelstein. The text was set in Granjon LT Std, and the display type was hand-lettered by Margaret Kimball.

The author acknowledges critical feedback from Arnaud Bessière, Alan Gordon, Janice Liedl, and David James Hudson; research assistance from Emma Stelter; and input about animal biology, behavior, and geographic range from Mathieson Smith.

ENCOUNTER

Written by Brittany Luby

Illustrated by Michaela Goade

LB

Little, Brown and Company

New York Boston

Sun rose to light all Creation.

He woke Seagull and Mouse from their nests.

He coaxed Mosquito from a long blade of grass.

He chuckled as Crab retreated inside her shell.

When the coastline buzzed with life, Sun woke the

two-leggeds with a burst of light.

This is Fisher. He tried to shoo Sun away by wiggling his toes.

So, Sun tickled Fisher's knees.

Fisher rolled onto his belly.

Sun persisted and gently warmed Fisher's neck.

Fisher woke, at last, to welcome the day ahead.

"I will paddle to waters thick with Mackerel," he said.

Fisher turned his canoe, loaded his nets, and pushed into the ocean.

This is Sailor. He came from away. He tried to block Sun by pulling a cap over his eyes.

Sun peeked through the fabric, knit with love. "Wake up, Sailor," Sun whispered.

At last, Sailor smiled. "Today, I will explore unknown lands in a new world."

Sailor lowered a boat from the ship. He rowed toward shore.

Sun had not traveled far when Fisher and Sailor paddled into the same bay.

Fisher knew the bay like the curve of his fingernail. But he did not know Sailor.

"Am I dreaming?" Fisher wondered. He rubbed his eyes. Sailor remained.

Sailor was puzzled too. "Perhaps these lands are not so new."

Both Sailor and Fisher hesitated, but the tide did not pause. It nudged them inland. Encouraged, they pulled their boats onto the rocky shore.

With his canoe secure, Fisher greeted Sailor, *"Kwe! Kwe!"*

Fisher watched Sailor's eyes open wide like Jellyfish.

"He speaks differently than me," Sailor thought. But he replied, *"Salut—Salutations!"*

Sailor watched Fisher's forehead wrinkle like an earthworm.

"We do not sound the same," Fisher thought. But he waved cautiously at Sailor.

"You are not so different," squawked Seagull, who flew overhead.
"You both cast long shadows."

Sailor tried to explain his journey across the water by drawing in the sand.

As Sailor sketched, his red wool cap fell to the ground.

Fisher laughed. He imagined Lobster had leapt off Sailor's head to scramble to the ocean.

The wind lifted Fisher's hair.

Sailor chuckled. He thought Fisher's hair looked like a horse's tail.

"You have much in common," Mosquito buzzed. "You both taste delicious!"

Sun now sat directly overhead and Sailor was getting hungry. His stomach grumbled.

Sailor pulled sea bread from his pocket. He gnawed at the edge before offering it to Fisher, who took a bite.

"I would rather chew wood!" Fisher thought, and returned the sea bread.

Fisher offered Sailor a handful of sunflower seeds. Sailor popped them into his mouth.

"I would rather eat pebbles!" he spat, peppering the ground with unopened seeds.

Fisher laughed. "You must crack open the shell."

Wordlessly, Fisher taught Sailor how to reach the heart of the seed.

Mouse was grateful for their crumbs. "Lucky me!" Mouse said. "A feast!"

Sun blazed west.

Sailor saw sweat beading on Fisher's chest.

"Does he not burn?" Sailor wondered. "He is almost bare."

Fisher watched sweat race down Sailor's temples from underneath his cap.

"Is he not boiling?" Fisher wondered. "He is heavily dressed."

Fisher pointed at the waves and Sailor beamed. Together, they jumped in.

Crab woke briefly to admire both swimmers. "What fine figures," Crab thought.

"They each found a shell to suit them."

Sailor and Fisher returned to shore where whistling in the bay alerted them that two beluga whales had come to play.

Fisher whistled back. Sailor too. They chased the whales along the shore.

"Good game! You'd make a strong pod," the belugas bellowed, and disappeared beneath the sparkling waves.

Before Sun fell, Sailor and Fisher parted with a sleepy smile.

Fisher set up camp. He unrolled a cedar mat under his canoe.

Fisher placed tobacco into the fire. He prayed for another friendly

encounter and lay down to rest.

Sailor returned to the ship. He pulled his straw mat onto the deck.

Sailor wished on a star for fewer chores and another chance to meet Fisher

before the long journey home.

Moon watched Sailor and Fisher fall asleep.

She shone on their ten fingers.

She shone on their ten toes.

Moon listened to their two hearts beat.

Ba-boom. Ba-boom.

She heard the beauty of all living things.

AUTHOR'S REFLECTION

I descend from the Anishinabeg. I did not inherit knowledge of Jacques Cartier's arrival from my ancestors. Cartier's history was left for me by settler-colonists—men from away who credited Cartier for claiming Indigenous territories for France. While my ancestral lands rest more than 1500 miles west of Gespe'gewa'gi (a territory occupied by the Mi'gmaq since time immemorial and now known as northern New Brunswick and the Gaspé Peninsula), Cartier's arrival would also affect my people. In 1608, Samuel de Champlain would build on Cartier's claim and establish a permanent settlement at Québec. As settlers' appetite for resources grew, so would the amount of land they took. By 1660, two French men—Médard Chouart des Groseilliers and Pierre-Esprit Radisson—entered Anishinaabe territory, linking France and its extractive industries to our fur-rich northlands.

It was because of this invasion that I learned about Jacques Cartier at school. Teachers told me that Cartier "discovered" parts of North America. My father disagreed. He said, "People have lived here since the world began." It is likely that a Stadaconan who knew the territory intimately would have greeted Cartier's men when they arrived. *Encounter* reminds us that Cartier and his crew were visitors here. They never permanently settled in North America. Teachers also taught me that Europeans like Cartier had "advanced technology," such as fully rigged ships with masts and sails. My father reminded me that knowledge is tied to place. Explorers may have sailed to North America, but they did not know how to live here. It is Indigenous, particularly Stadaconan, knowledge that is valued in this telling.

I wrote *Encounter* to provide an alter*native* view of Cartier's visit. This peaceful encounter does not forgive Jacques Cartier for his violent actions. Instead, it reminds us that violence is a choice. It also shows us that everyday people, like Sailor, can participate in systems that hurt others. By being a hand on Cartier's ship, Sailor helped to build a system that took resources from Indigenous peoples, like Fisher, and delivered them to Europeans.

Any of us could be like Sailor. It is vital to learn about where our food, water, and housing originate to ensure that we are not displacing others in serving ourselves.

HISTORICAL NOTE

Encounter is a work of imagination, but it is based on notes kept by Jacques Cartier, a real French explorer, on his first expedition to what is now known as North America. Cartier anchored his ship in what we now call Gaspé Bay, in 1534. While Mi'gmaq territory includes this region, records suggest that they shared fishing grounds with Stadaconans in the sixteenth century. In imagining an open and friendly meeting between a French sailor and a Stadaconan fisher, this story reminds us that in every encounter, there is the potential for common ground.

Unfortunately, when explorers arrived from Europe and observed that the land was already inhabited, many disrespected Indigenous peoples' claim to it. European invaders then used physical violence and European law to take Indigenous lands and resources for their countries of origin. Millions of their descendants continue to use stolen land.

And yet, according to Cartier, the earliest interactions between French sailors and Stadaconan fishers in 1534 were peaceful. Stadaconan families appear to have shared corn and fruit with the French crew. French sailors presented Stadaconan families with glass beads and other manufactured goods.

Relationships soured when Cartier captured two Stadaconan men, Domagaya and Taignoagny, in July 1534. He forced them to go with him to France. It is likely that Cartier used captives to improve his understanding of North American lands and waterways. About one year passed before Cartier returned these men to their families.

While we must reckon with this violent past and its hold on our present, the future is unchartered. May we learn from our history and take the opportunity to map a better future.